Monthly P

Month: ________ **Year:** ________

Monday	Tuesday	Wednesday	Thursday	Friday	Saturday	Sunday

Notes:

Monthly Planner

Month: ________ **Year:** ________

Monday	Tuesday	Wednesday	Thursday	Friday	Saturday	Sunday

Notes:

Monthly Planner

Month: ________ **Year:** ________

Monday	Tuesday	Wednesday	Thursday	Friday	Saturday	Sunday

Notes:

Monthly Planner

Month: ________ **Year:** ________

Monday	Tuesday	Wednesday	Thursday	Friday	Saturday	Sunday

Notes:

Monthly Planner

Month: ________ **Year:** ________

Monday	Tuesday	Wednesday	Thursday	Friday	Saturday	Sunday

Notes:

Monthly Planner

Month: ________ **Year:** ________

Monday	Tuesday	Wednesday	Thursday	Friday	Saturday	Sunday

Notes:

Monthly Planner

Month: ________ **Year:** ________

Monday	Tuesday	Wednesday	Thursday	Friday	Saturday	Sunday
☐	☐	☐	☐	☐	☐	☐
☐	☐	☐	☐	☐	☐	☐
☐	☐	☐	☐	☐	☐	☐
☐	☐	☐	☐	☐	☐	☐
☐	☐	☐	☐	☐	☐	☐

Notes:

Monthly Planner

Month: ________ **Year:** ________

Monday	Tuesday	Wednesday	Thursday	Friday	Saturday	Sunday

Notes:

Monthly Planner

Month: ________ **Year:** ________

Monday	Tuesday	Wednesday	Thursday	Friday	Saturday	Sunday

Notes:

Monthly Planner

Month: ________ **Year:** ________

Monday	Tuesday	Wednesday	Thursday	Friday	Saturday	Sunday

Notes:

Monthly Planner

Month: ________ **Year:** ________

Monday	Tuesday	Wednesday	Thursday	Friday	Saturday	Sunday

Notes:

Monthly Planner

Month: ________ **Year:** ________

Monday	Tuesday	Wednesday	Thursday	Friday	Saturday	Sunday

Notes:

Monthly Planner

Month: ________ **Year:** ________

Monday	Tuesday	Wednesday	Thursday	Friday	Saturday	Sunday

Notes:

Monthly Planner

Month: ________ **Year:** ________

Monday	Tuesday	Wednesday	Thursday	Friday	Saturday	Sunday

Notes:

Monthly Planner

Month: ________ **Year:** ________

Monday	Tuesday	Wednesday	Thursday	Friday	Saturday	Sunday

Notes:

Monthly Planner

Month: ________ Year: ________

Monday	Tuesday	Wednesday	Thursday	Friday	Saturday	Sunday

Notes:

Monthly Planner

Month: ________ **Year:** ________

Monday	Tuesday	Wednesday	Thursday	Friday	Saturday	Sunday

Notes:

Monthly Planner

Month: ________ Year: ________

Monday	Tuesday	Wednesday	Thursday	Friday	Saturday	Sunday

Notes:

Monthly Planner

Month: ________ **Year:** ________

Monday	Tuesday	Wednesday	Thursday	Friday	Saturday	Sunday

Notes:

Monthly Planner

Month: ________ **Year:** ________

Monday	Tuesday	Wednesday	Thursday	Friday	Saturday	Sunday

Notes:

Monthly Planner

Month: ________ **Year:** ________

Monday	Tuesday	Wednesday	Thursday	Friday	Saturday	Sunday

Notes:

Monthly Planner

Month: ________ **Year:** ________

Monday	Tuesday	Wednesday	Thursday	Friday	Saturday	Sunday

Notes:

Monthly Planner

Month: ________ **Year:** ________

Monday	Tuesday	Wednesday	Thursday	Friday	Saturday	Sunday

Notes:

Monthly Planner

Month: ________ Year: ________

Monday	Tuesday	Wednesday	Thursday	Friday	Saturday	Sunday

Notes:

Monthly Planner

Month: ________ **Year:** ________

Monday	Tuesday	Wednesday	Thursday	Friday	Saturday	Sunday

Notes:

Monthly Planner

Month: ________ **Year:** ________

Monday	Tuesday	Wednesday	Thursday	Friday	Saturday	Sunday

Notes:

Monthly Planner

Month: ________ **Year:** ________

Monday	Tuesday	Wednesday	Thursday	Friday	Saturday	Sunday

Notes:

Monthly Planner

Month: ________ **Year:** ________

Monday	Tuesday	Wednesday	Thursday	Friday	Saturday	Sunday

Notes:

Monthly Planner

Month: ________ **Year:** ________

Monday	Tuesday	Wednesday	Thursday	Friday	Saturday	Sunday

Notes:

Monthly Planner

Month: ______ **Year:** ______

Monday	Tuesday	Wednesday	Thursday	Friday	Saturday	Sunday

Notes:

Monthly Planner

Month: ________ **Year:** ________

Monday	Tuesday	Wednesday	Thursday	Friday	Saturday	Sunday

Notes:

Monthly Planner

Month: ________ Year: ________

Monday	Tuesday	Wednesday	Thursday	Friday	Saturday	Sunday

Notes:

Monthly Planner

Month: ________ **Year:** ________

Monday	Tuesday	Wednesday	Thursday	Friday	Saturday	Sunday

Notes:

Monthly Planner

Month: ________ **Year:** ________

Monday	Tuesday	Wednesday	Thursday	Friday	Saturday	Sunday

Notes:

Monthly Planner

Month: ________ **Year:** ________

Monday	Tuesday	Wednesday	Thursday	Friday	Saturday	Sunday

Notes:

Monthly Planner

Month: ________ **Year:** ________

Monday	Tuesday	Wednesday	Thursday	Friday	Saturday	Sunday

Notes:

Monthly Planner

Month: ________ **Year:** ________

Monday	Tuesday	Wednesday	Thursday	Friday	Saturday	Sunday

Notes:

Monthly Planner

Month: ________ **Year:** ________

Monday	Tuesday	Wednesday	Thursday	Friday	Saturday	Sunday

Notes:

Monthly Planner

Month: ________ **Year:** ________

Monday	Tuesday	Wednesday	Thursday	Friday	Saturday	Sunday

Notes:

Monthly Planner

Month: ________ **Year:** ________

Monday	Tuesday	Wednesday	Thursday	Friday	Saturday	Sunday

Notes:

Monthly Planner

Month: ________ **Year:** ________

Monday	Tuesday	Wednesday	Thursday	Friday	Saturday	Sunday

Notes:

Monthly Planner

Month: ________ **Year:** ________

Monday	Tuesday	Wednesday	Thursday	Friday	Saturday	Sunday

Notes:

Monthly Planner

Month: ________ **Year:** ________

Monday	Tuesday	Wednesday	Thursday	Friday	Saturday	Sunday

Notes:

Monthly Planner

Month: ________ **Year:** ________

Monday	Tuesday	Wednesday	Thursday	Friday	Saturday	Sunday
☐	☐	☐	☐	☐	☐	☐
☐	☐	☐	☐	☐	☐	☐
☐	☐	☐	☐	☐	☐	☐
☐	☐	☐	☐	☐	☐	☐
☐	☐	☐	☐	☐	☐	☐

Notes:

Monthly Planner

Month: ________ **Year:** ________

Monday	Tuesday	Wednesday	Thursday	Friday	Saturday	Sunday

Notes:

Monthly Planner

Month: ________ **Year:** ________

Monday	Tuesday	Wednesday	Thursday	Friday	Saturday	Sunday

Notes:

Monthly Planner

Month: ________ **Year:** ________

Monday	Tuesday	Wednesday	Thursday	Friday	Saturday	Sunday

Notes:

Monthly Planner

Month: ________ **Year:** ________

Monday	Tuesday	Wednesday	Thursday	Friday	Saturday	Sunday

Notes:

Monthly Planner

Month: ________ **Year:** ________

Monday	Tuesday	Wednesday	Thursday	Friday	Saturday	Sunday

Notes:

Monthly Planner

Month: ________ **Year:** ________

Monday	Tuesday	Wednesday	Thursday	Friday	Saturday	Sunday

Notes:

Monthly Planner

Month: ________ **Year:** ________

Monday	Tuesday	Wednesday	Thursday	Friday	Saturday	Sunday

Notes:

Monthly Planner

Month: ________ **Year:** ________

Monday	Tuesday	Wednesday	Thursday	Friday	Saturday	Sunday

Notes:

Monthly Planner

Month: ________ **Year:** ________

Monday	Tuesday	Wednesday	Thursday	Friday	Saturday	Sunday

Notes:

Monthly Planner

Month: ________ **Year:** ________

Monday	Tuesday	Wednesday	Thursday	Friday	Saturday	Sunday

Notes:

Monthly Planner

Month: ________ **Year:** ________

Monday	Tuesday	Wednesday	Thursday	Friday	Saturday	Sunday

Notes:

Monthly Planner

Month: ________ **Year:** ________

Monday	Tuesday	Wednesday	Thursday	Friday	Saturday	Sunday

Notes:

Monthly Planner

Month: ________ **Year:** ________

Monday	Tuesday	Wednesday	Thursday	Friday	Saturday	Sunday

Notes:

Monthly Planner

Month: ______ Year: ______

Monday	Tuesday	Wednesday	Thursday	Friday	Saturday	Sunday

Notes:

Monthly Planner

Month: ________ **Year:** ________

Monday	Tuesday	Wednesday	Thursday	Friday	Saturday	Sunday

Notes:

Monthly Planner

Month: ________ **Year:** ________

Monday	Tuesday	Wednesday	Thursday	Friday	Saturday	Sunday

Notes:

Monthly Planner

Month: ________ **Year:** ________

Monday	Tuesday	Wednesday	Thursday	Friday	Saturday	Sunday

Notes:

Monthly Planner

Month: ________ **Year:** ________

Monday	Tuesday	Wednesday	Thursday	Friday	Saturday	Sunday

Notes:

Monthly Planner

Month: ________ **Year:** ________

Monday	Tuesday	Wednesday	Thursday	Friday	Saturday	Sunday

Notes:

Monthly Planner

Month: ________ **Year:** ________

Monday	Tuesday	Wednesday	Thursday	Friday	Saturday	Sunday

Notes:

Monthly Planner

Month: ______ **Year:** ______

Monday	Tuesday	Wednesday	Thursday	Friday	Saturday	Sunday

Notes:

Monthly Planner

Month: ________ **Year:** ________

Monday	Tuesday	Wednesday	Thursday	Friday	Saturday	Sunday

Notes:

Monthly Planner

Month: ________ **Year:** ________

Monday	Tuesday	Wednesday	Thursday	Friday	Saturday	Sunday

Notes:

Monthly Planner

Month: ________ **Year:** ________

Monday	Tuesday	Wednesday	Thursday	Friday	Saturday	Sunday

Notes:

Monthly Planner

Month: ________ **Year:** ________

Monday	Tuesday	Wednesday	Thursday	Friday	Saturday	Sunday

Notes:

Monthly Planner

Month: ________ **Year:** ________

Monday	Tuesday	Wednesday	Thursday	Friday	Saturday	Sunday

Notes:

Monthly Planner

Month: ________ **Year:** ________

Monday	Tuesday	Wednesday	Thursday	Friday	Saturday	Sunday

Notes:

Monthly Planner

Month: ______ **Year:** ______

Monday	Tuesday	Wednesday	Thursday	Friday	Saturday	Sunday

Notes:

Monthly Planner

Month: ________ **Year:** ________

Monday	Tuesday	Wednesday	Thursday	Friday	Saturday	Sunday

Notes:

Monthly Planner

Month: ______ **Year:** ______

Monday	Tuesday	Wednesday	Thursday	Friday	Saturday	Sunday

Notes:

Monthly Planner

Month: ________ **Year:** ________

Monday	Tuesday	Wednesday	Thursday	Friday	Saturday	Sunday

Notes:

Monthly Planner

Month: ________ Year: ________

Monday	Tuesday	Wednesday	Thursday	Friday	Saturday	Sunday

Notes:

Monthly Planner

Month: ________ **Year:** ________

Monday	Tuesday	Wednesday	Thursday	Friday	Saturday	Sunday

Notes:

Monthly Planner

Month: ________ **Year:** ________

Monday	Tuesday	Wednesday	Thursday	Friday	Saturday	Sunday

Notes:

Monthly Planner

Month: ________ **Year:** ________

Monday	Tuesday	Wednesday	Thursday	Friday	Saturday	Sunday

Notes:

Monthly Planner

Month: ________ **Year:** ________

Monday	Tuesday	Wednesday	Thursday	Friday	Saturday	Sunday

Notes:

Monthly Planner

Month: ________ **Year:** ________

Monday	Tuesday	Wednesday	Thursday	Friday	Saturday	Sunday
☐	☐	☐	☐	☐	☐	☐
☐	☐	☐	☐	☐	☐	☐
☐	☐	☐	☐	☐	☐	☐
☐	☐	☐	☐	☐	☐	☐
☐	☐	☐	☐	☐	☐	☐

Notes:

Monthly Planner

Month: ________ **Year:** ________

Monday	Tuesday	Wednesday	Thursday	Friday	Saturday	Sunday

Notes:

Monthly Planner

Month: ________ **Year:** ________

Monday	Tuesday	Wednesday	Thursday	Friday	Saturday	Sunday

Notes:

Monthly Planner

Month: ________ **Year:** ________

Monday	Tuesday	Wednesday	Thursday	Friday	Saturday	Sunday

Notes:

Monthly Planner

Month: ________ Year: ________

Monday	Tuesday	Wednesday	Thursday	Friday	Saturday	Sunday

Notes:

Monthly Planner

Month: ______ **Year:** ______

Monday	Tuesday	Wednesday	Thursday	Friday	Saturday	Sunday
☐	☐	☐	☐	☐	☐	☐
☐	☐	☐	☐	☐	☐	☐
☐	☐	☐	☐	☐	☐	☐
☐	☐	☐	☐	☐	☐	☐
☐	☐	☐	☐	☐	☐	☐

Notes:

Monthly Planner

Month: ______ **Year:** ______

Monday	Tuesday	Wednesday	Thursday	Friday	Saturday	Sunday
☐	☐	☐	☐	☐	☐	☐
☐	☐	☐	☐	☐	☐	☐
☐	☐	☐	☐	☐	☐	☐
☐	☐	☐	☐	☐	☐	☐
☐	☐	☐	☐	☐	☐	☐

Notes:

Monthly Planner

Month: ________ **Year:** ________

Monday	Tuesday	Wednesday	Thursday	Friday	Saturday	Sunday
☐	☐	☐	☐	☐	☐	☐
☐	☐	☐	☐	☐	☐	☐
☐	☐	☐	☐	☐	☐	☐
☐	☐	☐	☐	☐	☐	☐
☐	☐	☐	☐	☐	☐	☐

Notes:

Monthly Planner

Month: ________ **Year:** ________

Monday	Tuesday	Wednesday	Thursday	Friday	Saturday	Sunday

Notes:

Monthly Planner

Month: ________ **Year:** ________

Monday	Tuesday	Wednesday	Thursday	Friday	Saturday	Sunday

Notes:

Monthly Planner

Month: ________ **Year:** ________

Monday	Tuesday	Wednesday	Thursday	Friday	Saturday	Sunday

Notes:

Monthly Planner

Month: ________ **Year:** ________

Monday	Tuesday	Wednesday	Thursday	Friday	Saturday	Sunday
☐	☐	☐	☐	☐	☐	☐
☐	☐	☐	☐	☐	☐	☐
☐	☐	☐	☐	☐	☐	☐
☐	☐	☐	☐	☐	☐	☐
☐	☐	☐	☐	☐	☐	☐

Notes:

Monthly Planner

Month: ________ **Year:** ________

Monday	Tuesday	Wednesday	Thursday	Friday	Saturday	Sunday

Notes:

Monthly Planner

Month: ________ **Year:** ________

Monday	Tuesday	Wednesday	Thursday	Friday	Saturday	Sunday

Notes:

Monthly Planner

Month: ________ **Year:** ________

Monday	Tuesday	Wednesday	Thursday	Friday	Saturday	Sunday

Notes:

Monthly Planner

Month: ________ **Year:** ________

Monday	Tuesday	Wednesday	Thursday	Friday	Saturday	Sunday

Notes:

Monthly Planner

Month: ________ **Year:** ________

Monday	Tuesday	Wednesday	Thursday	Friday	Saturday	Sunday

Notes:

Monthly Planner

Month: ________ **Year:** ________

Monday	Tuesday	Wednesday	Thursday	Friday	Saturday	Sunday

Notes:

Monthly Planner

Month: ________ **Year:** ________

Monday	Tuesday	Wednesday	Thursday	Friday	Saturday	Sunday

Notes:

Monthly Planner

Month: ________ **Year:** ________

Monday	Tuesday	Wednesday	Thursday	Friday	Saturday	Sunday

Notes:

Monthly Planner

Month: ________ **Year:** ________

Monday	Tuesday	Wednesday	Thursday	Friday	Saturday	Sunday

Notes:

Monthly Planner

Month: ________ **Year:** ________

Monday	Tuesday	Wednesday	Thursday	Friday	Saturday	Sunday

Notes:

Monthly Planner

Month: ________ **Year:** ________

Monday	Tuesday	Wednesday	Thursday	Friday	Saturday	Sunday

Notes:

Monthly Planner

Month: ________ **Year:** ________

Monday	Tuesday	Wednesday	Thursday	Friday	Saturday	Sunday

Notes:

Monthly Planner

Month: ________ **Year:** ________

Monday	Tuesday	Wednesday	Thursday	Friday	Saturday	Sunday
☐	☐	☐	☐	☐	☐	☐
☐	☐	☐	☐	☐	☐	☐
☐	☐	☐	☐	☐	☐	☐
☐	☐	☐	☐	☐	☐	☐
☐	☐	☐	☐	☐	☐	☐

Notes:

Monthly Planner

Month: ________ **Year:** ________

Monday	Tuesday	Wednesday	Thursday	Friday	Saturday	Sunday

Notes:

Monthly Planner

Month: ________ **Year:** ________

Monday	Tuesday	Wednesday	Thursday	Friday	Saturday	Sunday

Notes:

Monthly Planner

Month: ________ **Year:** ________

Monday	Tuesday	Wednesday	Thursday	Friday	Saturday	Sunday

Notes:

Monthly Planner

Month: ________ **Year:** ________

Monday	Tuesday	Wednesday	Thursday	Friday	Saturday	Sunday

Notes:

Monthly Planner

Month: ________ **Year:** ________

Monday	Tuesday	Wednesday	Thursday	Friday	Saturday	Sunday

Notes:

Made in the USA
Monee, IL
09 December 2021

84412711R00066